GIANT JIM
and TINY TIM

GIANT JIM
and TINY TIM

by JOYCE and JAMES DUNBAR

This is Tiny Tim.

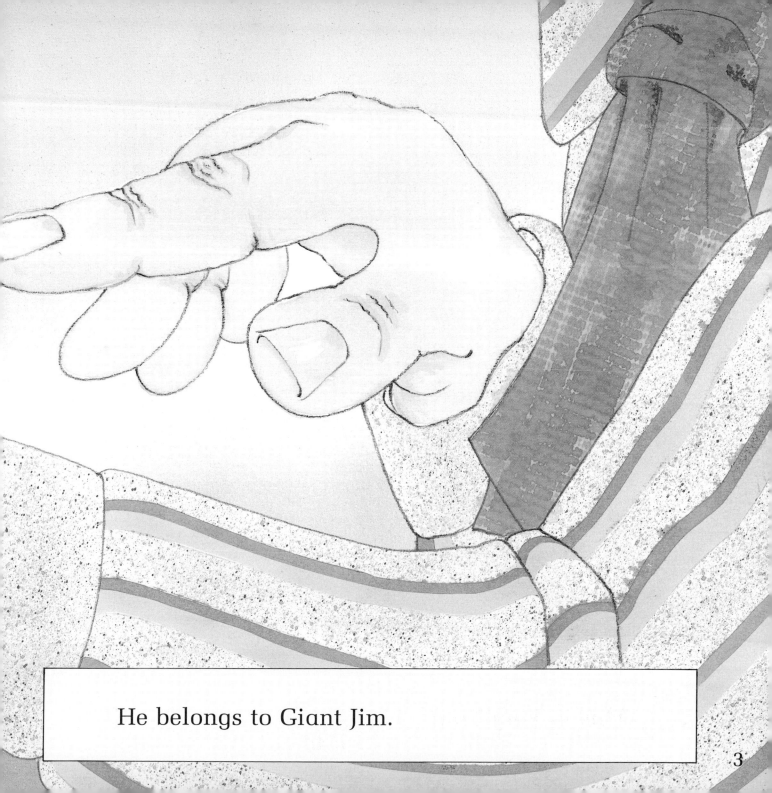

He belongs to Giant Jim.

3

Tiny Tim is in this book.
Giant Jim wants to be in it too . . .

. . . but he's much too big!

He tries to step in with his feet . . .

. . . but they are much too large!

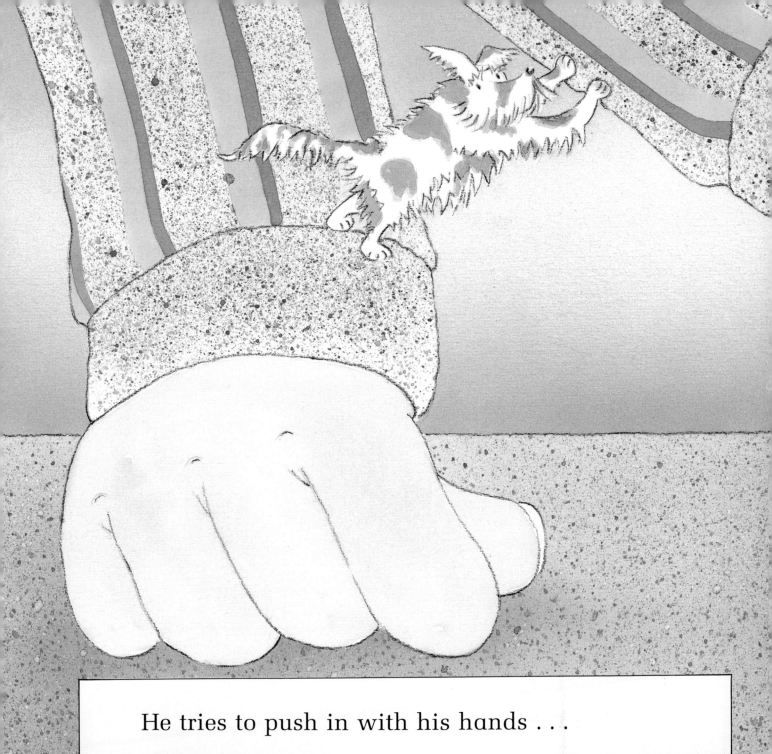

He tries to push in with his hands . . .

. . . but his arms are too long!

Now he's trying headfirst . . .

IMPOSSIBLE!

'I know what you should do,' said Tiny Tim,
'you must have the rest of the book to yourself.'

12

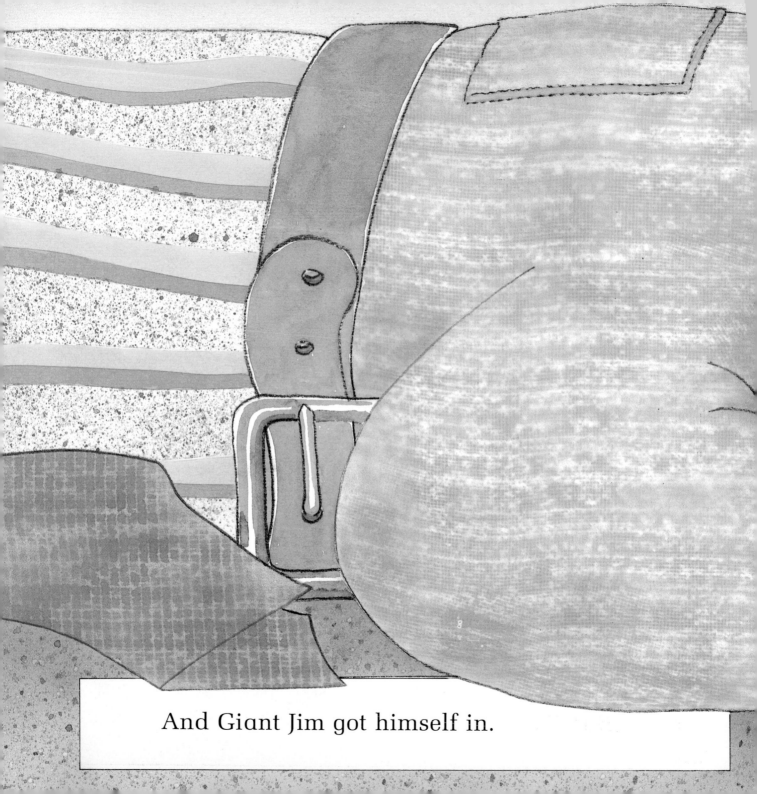

And Giant Jim got himself in.

. . . only just!

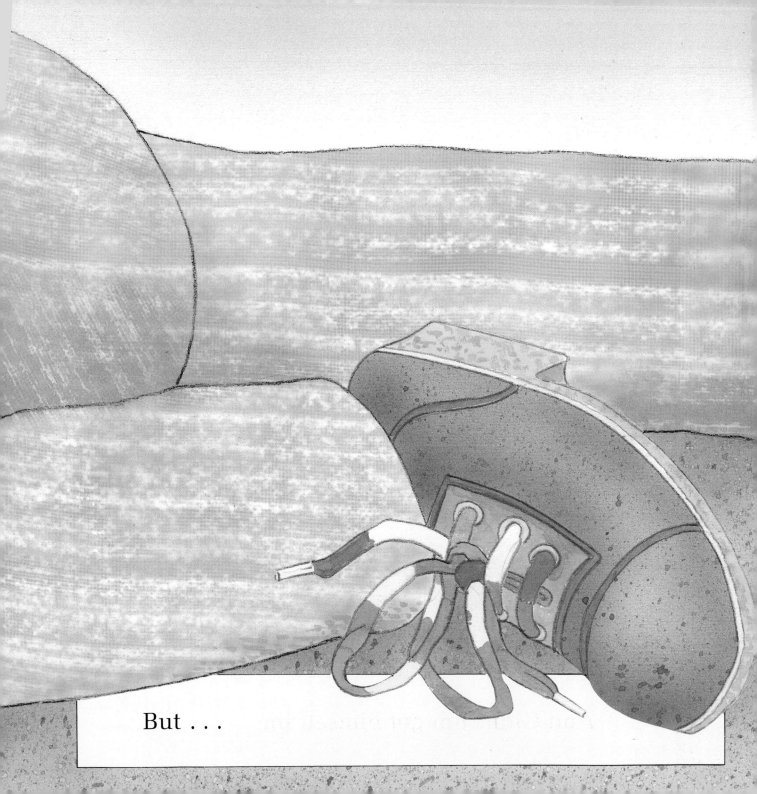

But . . .